BENNY'S FLAG

BENNY'S FLAG

story by *Phyllis Krasilovsky*

pictures by *W. T. Mars*

Cleveland and New York

THE WORLD PUBLISHING COMPANY

PUBLISHED BY The World Publishing Company
2231 West 110th Street, Cleveland 2, Ohio

PUBLISHED SIMULTANEOUSLY IN CANADA BY
Nelson, Foster & Scott Ltd.

Library of Congress Catalog Card Number: 60-5801

FIRST EDITION

To

Dorothy and Ernest Gruening	Bob and Doris Smithson
Evangeline and Bob Attwood	Dorothea and David Checkley
Amy and Bob Dale	Louise Brown
Ruthella Wade Caldwell	Bea and Ralph Browne
Mrs. Vera Bayers	Fred and Sara Machetanz
Jean and George Rogers	Alberta and Tex MacMurtrey
Kay and Lauris Parker	Molly Tryck
Peggy MacIver	Daphne and Barrie White, Jr.
Bill and Ione Paul	Dotty and Mike Ozkus
Rie Mounier Munoz	Mr. and Mrs. Cline Koonz
Lorene and Jack Harrison	Anne and Spence Delong
Ruth Beckmann	Lola and Art Kahn
Mary and Emil Kientz	Judge George W. Folta
Bob and Doris Smith	Judge Anthony Dimond

Mayor and Mrs. "Zach" Loussac

the stars and forget-me-nots of our Alaska

Benny was an Indian boy who lived in Alaska
many years before it became a state. He had
straight black hair and bright black eyes, but
best of all he had the whitest white teeth and a
happy, friendly smile. Everyone liked Benny, for

Benny liked everyone. He had no father and mother, but he had many, many friends in the mission home where he lived. That was a place for boys and girls who had no families.

The children ate together in a big dining room. They slept in big rooms, called dormitories, which had many beds in them. And in the winter they all went to the same school that the other children in the village attended.

Benny was happy in the mission home. But sometimes before he went to sleep at night, he would gaze at the stars outside his dormitory window and long for the day when he would be a grown-up man. For then he was going to be a fine fisherman. He would use a big net like the Big Dipper to catch splendid silver fish. And like the Big Dipper, which was really a great strong bear of night, he would be big and strong himself. The North Star would guide his boat, for the North Star is the star of Alaska, the northernmost state in America.

Sometimes, when the sky was scattered with hundreds of stars, it reminded Benny of a field of forget-me-nots, the little star-shaped flowers which grow wild everywhere. The blue sky was a roof that covered Benny's Alaska at night.

In the summertime, when only the mountain-tops were still covered with snow, Benny enjoyed himself on picnics with the other mission children. Sometimes he went swimming, too, though the water was often cold.

One lucky day a kind fisherman took Benny fishing with him in his boat. Almost at once Benny caught a big silver salmon all by himself. It was so big that there was enough for everyone at the mission house to eat for supper, and everyone said it was delicious.

Benny was so happy he could hardly sleep that night. He lay awake looking at the stars, dreaming his dream of becoming a real fisherman. The Big Dipper looked more like a great strong bear than ever because Benny felt so big and strong himself!

When fall came, school started again just as it does for children everywhere. But then the winter came quickly, far more quickly than it does anywhere else. The first snowy day Benny went to school wearing a parka, which is a fur-hooded jacket, and mukluks, which are fur-lined boots, and thick mittens to keep his fingers warm. He looked more like a furry bear than an Indian boy!

As he walked along the snow-covered road he wondered if all the little blue forget-me-not flowers which covered the fields in summer were now growing under the earth. In the cold winter

sunshine the world was all white-and-twinkly
snow. The silver fish had gone downstream to
warmer places; and the fishing boats, anchored
near the beach, looked like a fleet of ghost ships.

That day in school the teacher told the children that there was a contest to make a flag for Alaska. With all his heart Benny wanted to win the contest. He thought how grand it would be to see his flag carried in a parade or hung on the mission-house flagpole on holidays or flying at the masts of big ships that came to the village in the summertime. He thought how especially grand it would be to see his flag flying on the fishing boat he would have one day.

That night the boys and girls at the mission house collected crayons, paints, and paper, and made many, many designs for the flag. They sat around a big table and as they worked they talked and laughed and sometimes held up their designs for the others to see. But Benny sat quietly, thinking and thinking. For once no one could see his white teeth and happy, friendly smile. He was thinking of what he loved the most about Alaska.

Some of the children drew pictures of the beautiful snow-covered mountains in Alaska.

Some drew pictures of the big fish that can be caught in Alaska. Some drew pictures of the northern lights that sometimes cross Alaskan skies.

Some drew pictures of the Alaskan forests.

Some drew pictures of the Alaskan glaciers, and
some drew pictures of the Alaskan rivers. And
some drew star designs or stripe designs or plaid
designs or flower designs.

Suddenly Benny knew what he wanted his flag to be like. He wanted his flag to be like the stars he dreamed by—gold stars spread out like the Big Dipper in the blue sky. So that is what he painted. And underneath it he wrote: "The blue field is for the Alaska sky and the forget-me-not, an Alaskan flower. The North Star is for the future state of Alaska, the most northerly of the Union. The dipper is for the Great Bear—symbolizing strength."

Benny didn't show his paper to anyone. He was too shy. He thought the other children's designs were much better than his. Still, the next day he gave his paper to the teacher when she collected the others.

A month went by and the teacher didn't mention the contest again. Benny ice-skated and had snowball fights and went sleigh-riding with the other children. And so the winter went quickly by.

And suddenly the snow and ice began to melt. Benny no longer wore his parka and mukluks and mittens. He began to watch for the forget-me-nots in the drying fields as he walked to school.

He watched the fishermen mend their nets for the coming fishing season. He watched the world change from white to green.

Then, one day, when school was almost over, the teacher called the children together. "Children," she said, "the flag contest is ended. From all over Alaska boys and girls sent in designs for the flag. From northern Nome

to the busy cities of Anchorage and Fairbanks,

from the fishing towns of Seward and Petersburg,

to Juneau, the capital,

and the lumber town of Ketchikan...

from everywhere came hundreds of designs. And
... Boys and girls! *Benny's* design won the contest! From now on, *Benny's* design will be Alaska's
flag!"

What a proud and happy boy Benny was! And
what an especially proud and happy boy he was
on the Fourth of July. For on that day there was
a big parade in the village to celebrate the holi-

day. Everyone came to see the parade—to see the marchers with their drums and fifes, to see the bright uniforms, to see the baton twirlers, to see the banners. . . . But the very first thing they saw

was BENNY.... Benny marching at the head of the parade, carrying the flag he had made for the fishing boat he would have, carrying the flag he had made for Alaska!

This is a true story!

BENNY BENSON was thirteen years old and a seventh-grade pupil in the Territorial school at Seward when the Alaska Flag Contest was launched in October, 1926. This contest was open to all Alaskan school children enrolled in grades seven to twelve. Benny's design was chosen by the Territorial legislature from 142 designs submitted, and it was adopted as Alaska's official flag in May, 1927. The first flag is still on display in the Territorial Museum at Juneau, and now that Alaska is a state, it continues as the official state flag. Benny himself grew up to be a fine fisherman, fishing off the southeastern coast of Alaska.

ABOUT THE AUTHOR

PHYLLIS KRASILOVSKY first heard of Benny and his flag when she lived in Alaska several years ago. She and her husband, a young attorney just out of law school, traveled up the Alcan Highway in a small foreign car and worked their way through the Territory one summer previous to settling there for the following three years. A picture of Benny and his design for Alaska's flag in the Territorial Museum in Juneau "arrested my attention," she says. "It seemed to me such a thrilling thing for a child to do, to design a flag for the whole gigantic Territory!"

Mrs. Krasilovsky is the author of several children's books, of which the most recent are *Scaredy Cat* (Macmillan) and *The Cow Who Fell in the Canal* (Doubleday). She and her husband and three daughters now live in Chappaqua, New York, but "the beauty and variety of Alaska still haunts us," and they hope someday to revisit what their oldest daughter, who was born in Juneau, calls "her country."